U0098870

 This ***book*** belongs to:

_____

Leon Gets a Scarecut

Text©Alan MacDonald 1998

Illustrations©Sally-Anne Lambert 1998

First published in Great Britain in 1998 by

Macdonald Young Books

李恩剪髮記

Alan MacDonald 著

Sally-Anne Lambert 繪

張憶萍 譯

三民書局

Leon **woke** up feeling excited. It was
Patsy's party this afternoon and he was
invited. He **rushed** downstairs for breakfast
and **bumped into** his mum.

"Oh Leon! Do look where you're going!"

李ㄌㄧˇ恩ㄣ一ㄧˋ早ㄗㄠˇ興ㄒㄧㄥ奮ㄈㄣˋ地ㄉㄧˋ起ㄑㄧˇ床ㄔㄨㄤˊ，他ㄊㄚ被ㄅㄟˋ邀ㄧㄠ請ㄑㄧㄥˇ參ㄘㄢ加ㄐㄧㄚ今ㄐㄧㄣ天ㄊㄧㄢ下ㄒㄧㄚˋ午ㄨˇ佩ㄆㄟˋ琪ㄑㄧˊ的ㄉㄜ派ㄆㄞˋ對ㄉㄨㄟˋ呢ㄋㄜ！他ㄊㄚ衝ㄔㄨㄥ下ㄒㄧㄚˋ樓ㄌㄡˊ去ㄑㄩˋ吃ㄔ早ㄗㄠˇ餐ㄘㄢ時ㄕˊ，撞ㄓㄨㄤˋ到ㄉㄠˋ了ㄌㄜ媽ㄇㄚ媽ㄇㄚ。

　　「喔ㄛ！李ㄌㄧˇ恩ㄣ！要ㄧㄠˋ看ㄎㄢˋ路ㄌㄨˋ啊ㄚ！」

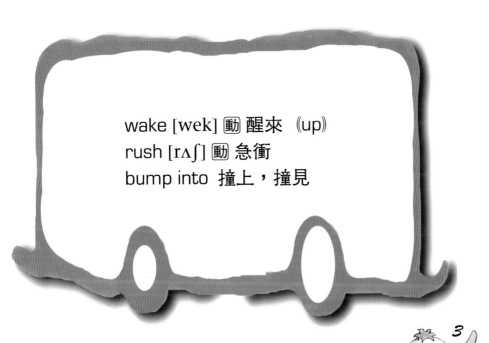

wake [wek] 動 醒來 《up》
rush [rʌʃ] 動 急衝
bump into 撞上，撞見

"Sorry Mum," said Leon, **brushing** his **mane** out of his eyes.

He sat down for breakfast.

"What you need is a **haircut**, Leon," said his mum. "You can't go to Patsy's party like that. You look like a **haystack**."

「對不起啦！媽。」李恩邊說，邊把頭髮從眼前撥開。

他坐下來吃早餐。

「李恩，你得剪頭髮了！」媽媽說。你不能這樣子去參加佩琪的派對，你的頭髮看起來像堆稻草呢！」

brush [brʌʃ] 動 梳理
mane [men] 名 （像鬃毛一樣）
　又長又密的頭髮
haircut [`hɛr͵kʌt] 名 理髮；髮型
haystack [`he͵stæk] 名 乾草堆

5

"**H**umph!" **grunted** Leon. He hated
having his hair cut.

Sid's **Barbershop** was in the **high street**.
On the way there Leon met his friend Ben.

「哼ㄥ！」李ㄌㄧˇ恩ㄣ嘟ㄉㄨ嚷ㄖㄤˇ著ㄓㄜ。他ㄊㄚ討ㄊㄠˇ厭ㄧㄢˋ剪ㄐㄧㄢ頭ㄊㄡˊ髮ㄈㄚˇ。

席ㄒㄧˊ德ㄉㄜˊ理ㄌㄧˇ髮ㄈㄚˇ店ㄉㄧㄢˋ在ㄗㄞˋ大ㄉㄚˋ街ㄐㄧㄝ上ㄕㄤˋ。在ㄗㄞˋ去ㄑㄩˋ理ㄌㄧˇ髮ㄈㄚˇ店ㄉㄧㄢˋ的ㄉㄜ路ㄌㄨˋ上ㄕㄤˋ，李ㄌㄧˇ恩ㄣ遇ㄩˋ見ㄐㄧㄢˋ了ㄌㄜ他ㄊㄚ的ㄉㄜ朋ㄆㄥˊ友ㄧㄡˇ小ㄒㄧㄠˇ班ㄅㄢ。

---

humph [hʌmf] 感 哼

grunt [grʌnt] 動 嘟嚷

barbershop [`barbɚˌʃɑp] 名 理髮店

high street　大街

7

"Hello Ben," said Leon. "Is that a new hat?"

"Yes, it's for Patsy's party," said Ben.

Leon wanted to say he was going to the party too.

「嗨！小班。」李恩說。「你戴的是新帽子嗎？」

「是啊！為了參加佩琪的派對呀！」小班說。

李恩本來想說他也要去參加派對的。

But he didn't get the chance. Ben had gone.

Bye Ben!
再見，小班！

Round the corner, they bumped into Guy and his dad.

10

可是他還沒機會說，小班就已經走掉了。

在轉角的地方，李恩和媽媽遇到了阿凱和他爸爸。

11

"**H**i Guy! You've got a hat too!"
"Dad **bought** it for me. I'm going to
wear it to Patsy's party," Guy told them.

"I didn't know it was a hat party," said
Leon.

「嗨！阿凱。你也有頂帽子啊！」

「這是我爸爸買給我的。我要戴著這頂帽子去參加佩琪的派對。」阿凱告訴他們說。

「我不知道這是個帽子派對啊！」李恩說。

buy [baɪ] 勯 買
（過去式 bought [bɔt]）
wear [wɛr] 勯 穿戴

13

"It isn't," said Guy, **blushing**. "Come on, Dad, let's look in here."

He **dashed** into a toy shop, **dragging** his dad with him.

Leon saw another of his friends. Felix was coming out of Helen's Hat Shop.

「不是帽子派對啦！」阿凱紅著臉說。「快點兒，老爸，我們進去看看！」

他拖著爸爸很快跑進一家玩具店。

李恩看到另一個朋友菲立斯。他正從海倫帽店走出來。

blush [blʌʃ] 動 臉紅
dash [dæʃ] 動 疾走
drag [dræg] 動 拖

Felix's mum had

bought him a new baseball cap.

    "Hello, Felix. I like your hat.

I **bet** it's for Patsy's party."

    "How did you know?" asked Felix.

    "Everyone I meet seems to be wearing

                 hats today."

16

"Really? Well I've got to go. See you, Leon!" Felix **waved** and ran off to the **bus stop**.

"Why is everyone in such a **rush** today?" thought Leon.

菲立斯的媽媽替他買了一頂新的棒球帽。

「嗨！菲立斯，我喜歡你的帽子喲！我打賭這是為了參加佩琪的派對吧！」

「你怎麼知道啊？」菲立斯問。

「我今天遇到的每個人好像都有戴帽子。」

「真的嗎？嗯！我得走了，再見，李恩！」菲立斯揮了揮手，然後跑向公車站。

「為什麼今天大家都急急忙忙的呢？」李恩心想。

bet [bɛt] 動 打賭
wave [wev] 動 揮手
bus stop　公車招呼站
rush [rʌʃ] 名 匆忙

They arrived at Sid's Barber shop.

"Good morning!" said Sid. "What can I do for you?"

他們來到了席德理髮店。

「早安！」席德說。「要剪頭髮嗎？」

"Leon needs a haircut," said Leon's Mum. "He's going to a party this afternoon and his mane is a **mess**. Can you **tidy** it up, please?"

Leon sat in Sid's big black chair **in front of** the **mirror**.

「李恩要剪頭髮。」李恩的媽媽說。「他今天下午要參加一個派對，可是他的頭髮卻一團亂呢！麻煩你幫他整理一下，好嗎？」

李恩坐在席德那黑色的大椅子上，面對著鏡子。

mess [mɛs] 名 一團亂
tidy [`taɪdɪ] 動 整理 《up》
in front of 在…前面
mirror [`mɪrɚ] 名 鏡子

21

"**D**on't worry," said Sid. "My new
electric trimmer will do the **trick**. It cuts
hair in half the time."

Leon felt a bit **nervous** as Sid **set to**
work.

「別擔心！」席德說。「我這把新的電動剪髮器會玩把戲呢！剪髮只要以前一半的時間就夠了。」

席德要動手剪了，李恩有點兒緊張。

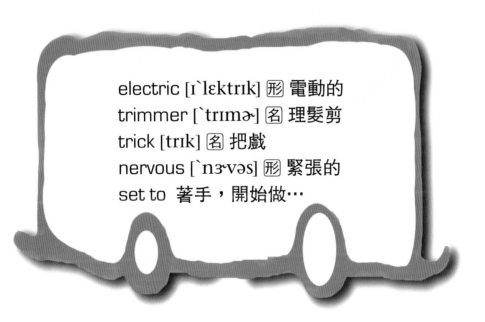

electric [ɪ`lɛktrɪk] 形 電動的
trimmer [`trɪmɚ] 名 理髮剪
trick [trɪk] 名 把戲
nervous [`nɝvəs] 形 緊張的
set to 著手，開始做…

23

The trimmer **buzzed** in his ears.
Leon closed his eyes until it was over.

At last Sid **turned off** the trimmer.
Leon opened his eyes and looked at
himself in the mirror.

24

電ㄉㄧㄢˋ動ㄉㄨㄥˋ剪ㄐㄧㄢˇ髮ㄈㄚˇ器ㄑㄧˋ在ㄗㄞˋ他ㄊㄚ耳ㄦˇ邊ㄅㄧㄢ嗡ㄨㄥ嗡ㄨㄥ地ㄉㄜˋ叫ㄐㄧㄠˋ。

李ㄌㄧˇ恩ㄣ閉ㄅㄧˋ著ㄓㄜˋ眼ㄧㄢˇ睛ㄐㄧㄥ直ㄓˊ到ㄉㄠˋ頭ㄊㄡˊ髮ㄈㄚˇ剪ㄐㄧㄢˇ完ㄨㄢˊ為ㄨㄟˊ止ㄓˇ。

席ㄒㄧˊ德ㄉㄜˊ終ㄓㄨㄥ於ㄩˊ把ㄅㄚˇ電ㄉㄧㄢˋ動ㄉㄨㄥˋ剪ㄐㄧㄢˇ髮ㄈㄚˇ器ㄑㄧˋ關ㄍㄨㄢ掉ㄉㄧㄠˋ了ㄌㄜ。

李ㄌㄧˇ恩ㄣ睜ㄓㄥ開ㄎㄞ眼ㄧㄢˇ睛ㄐㄧㄥ，看ㄎㄢˋ了ㄌㄜ看ㄎㄢˋ鏡ㄐㄧㄥˋ中ㄓㄨㄥ的ㄉㄜ自ㄗˋ己ㄐㄧˇ。

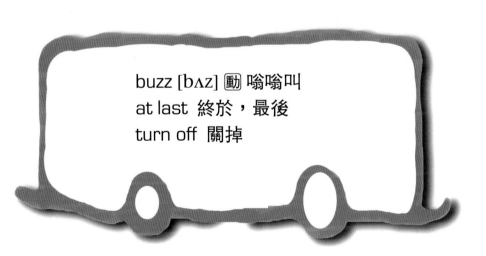

buzz [bʌz] 動 嗡嗡叫
at last 終於，最後
turn off 關掉

Oh, no!
哦！天哪！

"What have you done to him?" **gasped** Leon's mum.

"Sorry," said Sid. "I got a bit **carried away**. Did I cut it too short?"

"Short?" cried Leon.

"I look like a **hedgehog!**" His long, thick mane had been cut to tiny **spikes**.

26

「你把他怎麼了？」李恩的媽媽緊張的問。

「抱歉啦！」席德回答說：「我有點太投入了，是不是剪得太短了呢？」

「何止短？」李恩大叫了起來。

「我看起來像隻刺蝟！」他那又長又密的頭髮現在變成了細細小小的尖刺。

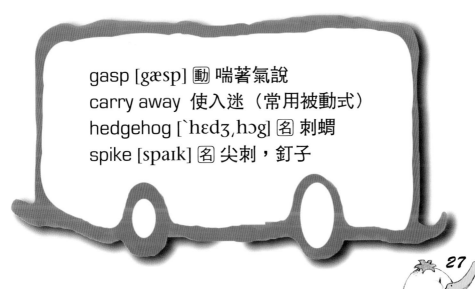

gasp [gæsp] 動 喘著氣說
carry away 使入迷（常用被動式）
hedgehog [`hɛdʒ,hɔg] 名 刺蝟
spike [spaɪk] 名 尖刺，釘子

Leon walked
close **behind** his mum
on the way home.
He hoped **none**
of his friends saw
him. They might **laugh at** his funny haircut.
His mum tried to **cheer** him **up**.

"**Never mind**, Leon, you've still got Patsy's party this afternoon."

"I'm not going! I can't go anywhere looking like this!" **moaned** Leon.

回家的路上，李恩緊緊地跟在媽媽身後。

　　李恩不希望被他的朋友看到，他們可能會嘲笑他這個滑稽的髮型呢！

　　李恩的媽媽努力想讓他心情好一點兒。

behind [bɪ`haɪnd] 介 在…後面
none [nʌn] 名 沒有一人
laugh at 嘲笑
cheer...up 使（某人）高興

「沒關係的，李恩，下午還有佩琪的派對啊！」

「我不要去了！我這個樣子，哪兒也去不成！」李恩發著牢騷。

mind [maɪnd] 働 介意
Never mind! 沒關係
moan [mon] 働 發牢騷

Just then they passed Helen's Hat Shop.
It gave Leon's mum an idea.

"Hello Helen, I want to buy a hat. Leon
needs one for Patsy's party this afternoon."

"That's funny," said Helen. "Everyone
wants a hat today. I've **nearly sold out**."

Leon stood and **sulked** while Helen
looked for a hat.

就在這個時候，他們經過海倫帽店。

這讓李恩的媽媽靈機一動。

「妳好啊！海倫，我想買一頂帽子。李恩需要一頂帽子去參加下午佩琪的派對。」

「可真是有意思啊！」海倫說。「大家今天都來買帽子，我的帽子幾乎快賣光囉！」

海倫在找帽子，而李恩繃著張臉站在那兒。

nearly [ˋnɪrlɪ] 副 幾乎
sell [sɛl] 動 賣
　（過去式 sold [sold]）
sell out 賣光
sulk [sʌlk] 動
　（生氣）繃著臉

33

At last she found one. It had **flaps** to **cover** Leon's ears.

Leon looked in the mirror. He thought the hat looked good and, best of all, no one would see his haircut.

最後她找到了一頂側邊有垂耳的帽子，這正好可以遮住李恩的耳朵。

李恩照了照鏡子，他覺得這頂帽子看起來不錯；最大的好處是，沒有人看得到他新剪的髮型。

flap [flæp] 名 垂下的帽緣
cover [ˋkʌvɚ] 動 遮住

All
Leon's friends were at Patsy's party.

It was a **bright**, **breezy** day, so they were playing in the back garden.

36

李恩全部的朋友都參加了佩琪的派對。

因為天氣晴朗，又吹著微風，大夥兒就在後院裡玩耍。

bright [braɪt] 形 晴朗的
breezy [`brizɪ] 形 有微風的

37

"Hello there, Leon," said Patsy's mum.
"What a **smart** hat! Shall I take it for you?" "No thank you," he said. "I'll keep it on." Leon **held on to** his hat **tightly**.

Guy, Ben and Felix were all playing **chase**.

Leon saw they were all wearing their new hats.

「你ㄋㄧˇ好ㄏㄠˇ啊ㄚ！李ㄌㄧˇ恩ㄣ。」佩ㄆㄟˋ琪ㄑㄧˊ的ㄉㄜ媽ㄇㄚ媽ㄇㄚ說ㄕㄨㄛ。

「好ㄏㄠˇ帥ㄕㄨㄞˋ的ㄉㄜ帽ㄇㄠˋ子ㄗ˙呀ㄚ！要ㄧㄠˋ不ㄅㄨˋ要ㄧㄠˋ我ㄨㄛˇ替ㄊㄧˋ你ㄋㄧˇ拿ㄋㄚˊ著ㄓㄜ˙？」「不ㄅㄨˋ用ㄩㄥˋ了ㄌㄜ˙，謝ㄒㄧㄝˋ謝ㄒㄧㄝˋ妳ㄋㄧˇ。」李ㄌㄧˇ恩ㄣ說ㄕㄨㄛ。「我ㄨㄛˇ戴ㄉㄞˋ著ㄓㄜ˙就ㄐㄧㄡˋ好ㄏㄠˇ了ㄌㄜ˙。」李ㄌㄧˇ恩ㄣ緊ㄐㄧㄣˇ緊ㄐㄧㄣˇ地ㄉㄜ˙抓ㄓㄨㄚ著ㄓㄜ˙他ㄊㄚ的ㄉㄜ帽ㄇㄠˋ子ㄗ˙。

阿ㄚ凱ㄎㄞˇ、小ㄒㄧㄠˇ班ㄅㄢ和ㄏㄜˊ菲ㄈㄟ立ㄌㄧˋ斯ㄙ在ㄗㄞˋ那ㄋㄚˇ兒ㄦ˙追ㄓㄨㄟ來ㄌㄞˊ追ㄓㄨㄟ去ㄑㄩˋ。

李ㄌㄧˇ恩ㄣ看ㄎㄢˋ到ㄉㄠˋ他ㄊㄚ們ㄇㄣ˙都ㄉㄡ戴ㄉㄞˋ著ㄓㄜ˙自ㄗˋ己ㄐㄧˇ的ㄉㄜ新ㄒㄧㄣ帽ㄇㄠˋ子ㄗ˙。

Hello Leon, come and join in!
嗨！李恩，一起來玩吧！

smart [smart] 形 時髦的
hold on to... 緊緊抓住…
tightly [`taɪtlɪ] 副 緊緊地
chase [tʃes] 名 追趕

Guy
chased them
all round the garden.

He caught Leon. Just then a big **gust** of wind **blew**. It **lifted** their hats right off and blew them away.

Leon blushed to his **spiky roots**.
He **waited** for his friends to
laugh at his haircut. But
nobody did.

Guy, Ben and Felix **stared** at each other
in **surprise**.

All of them had the same haircut.

阿ㄚ凱ㄞ繞ㄖㄠˋ著ㄓㄜ˙後ㄏㄡˋ院ㄩㄢˋ追ㄓㄨㄟ他ㄊㄚ們ㄇㄣ˙。

他ㄊㄚ抓ㄓㄨㄚ到ㄉㄠˋ了ㄌㄜ˙李ㄌㄧˇ恩ㄣ。就ㄐㄧㄡˋ在ㄗㄞˋ這ㄓㄜˋ時ㄕˊ候ㄏㄡˋ，刮ㄍㄨㄚ起ㄑㄧˇ了ㄌㄜ˙一一ˊ陣ㄓㄣˋ強ㄑㄧㄤˊ風ㄈㄥ，正ㄓㄥˋ巧ㄑㄧㄠˇ把ㄅㄚˇ他ㄊㄚ們ㄇㄣ˙的ㄉㄜ˙帽ㄇㄠˋ子ㄗ˙掀ㄒㄧㄢ起ㄑㄧˇ吹ㄔㄨㄟ走ㄗㄡˇ。

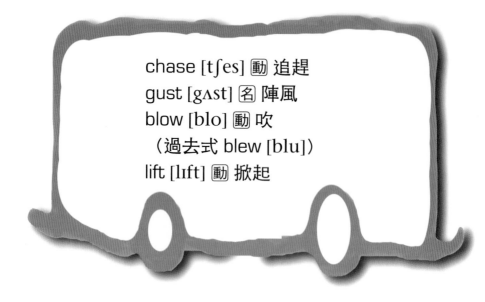

chase [tʃes] 勔 追趕
gust [gʌst] 图 陣風
blow [blo] 勔 吹
　（過去式 blew [blu]）
lift [lɪft] 勔 掀起

李恩羞愧得滿臉通紅。

他等著朋友嘲笑他的髮型，可是居然沒有人嘲笑他呢！

阿凱、小班和菲立斯驚訝地互相看著。

他們全都剪了一模一樣的髮型啊！

spiky [`spaɪkɪ] 形 尖尖的
root [rut] 名（髮）根
wait [wet] 動 等待《for》
stare [stɛr] 動 盯著看《at》
surprise [sə`praɪz] 名 驚訝

"I know where you've all been,"
laughed Leon, "to Sid's Barbershop. And
you all got a scarecut-haircut like me!"

44

「我知道你們去過哪裡喲！」李恩笑著說：「你們都去了席德理髮店！而且你們都和我一樣剪了一個嚇人的髮型！」

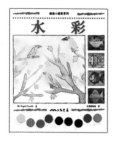

創意小畫家系列

榮獲 聯合報《讀書人》版年度最佳童書！

——由西班牙Parramón ediciones,S.A.獨家授權出版

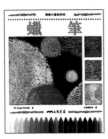

當一個天才小畫家
發揮想像力
讓色彩和線條在紙上跳起舞來！！

藝術叢書

一共15本，教你怎麼用面紙拼貼、
畫各種風景、動物，
還有冰淇淋哦！！

每天一段奇遇、一個狂想、一則幽默的小故事
365天．讓你天天笑開懷！

中英對照喔！！

伍史利的
大日記 I、II
—— 哈洛森林的妙生活

Linda Hayward 著／三民書局編輯部譯

有一天，一隻叫做伍史利的大熊來到一個叫做「哈洛小森林」的地方，並決定要為這森林寫一本書，這就是《伍史利的大日記》！

你看，青蛙爸爸正在為他九百九十八個蝌蚪寶寶取名而傷腦筋，而浣熊洛奇則是為媽媽做情人節蛋糕……日記裡的每一天都有一段歷險記或溫馨有趣的小故事，不管你從哪天開始讀，保證都會有意想不到的驚喜哦！

國家圖書館出版品預行編目資料

李恩剪髮記 = Leon gets a scarecut / Alan MacDonald
　著；Sally-Anne Lambert 繪；張憶萍譯－－初版.
　－－臺北市：三民，民88
　　面；　公分
　ISBN 957-14-3005-6（平裝）

1.英國語言－讀本

805.18　　　　　　　　　　　　　88004016

網際網路位址　http://www.sanmin.com.tw

ⓒ 李恩剪髮記

著作人　Alan MacDonald
繪圖者　Sally-Anne Lambert
譯　者　張憶萍
發行人　劉振強
著作財　三民書局股份有限公司
產權人
　　　　臺北市復興北路三八六號
發行所　三民書局股份有限公司
　　　　地址／臺北市復興北路三八六號
　　　　電話／二五〇〇六六〇〇
　　　　郵撥／〇〇〇九九九八－－五號
印刷所　三民書局股份有限公司
門市部　復北店／臺北市復興北路三八六號
　　　　重南店／臺北市重慶南路一段六十一號
初　版　中華民國八十八年九月
編　號　S85476
定　價　新臺幣壹佰壹拾元整
行政院新聞局登記證局版臺業字第〇二〇〇號

有著作權　不准侵害

ISBN　957-14-3005-6（平裝）